Alphabeast Soup

Written, designed, and illustrated by

Andy Hopp

ALPHABEAST SOUP
Copyright (c) 2015 by Andy Hopp
All rights reserved. Manufactured in the USA by Mutha Oith Creations, Green, Ohio.
Printed in the USA by Josten's Commercial Printing, Clarksville TN
No part of this book may be reproduced in any manner whatsoever without written permission except in the case of brief quotations embodied in critical articles and reviews.
For information please address Mutha Oith Creations, 1700 Steese Road, Uniontown, OH 44685

Library of Congress Control Number: 2015910267
ISBN 978-0-9856591-2-7

ALPHABEAST SOUP: LIMITED COLLECTOR'S EDITION
WWW.MUTHAOITHCREATIONS.COM

For
Iliana and Aurora

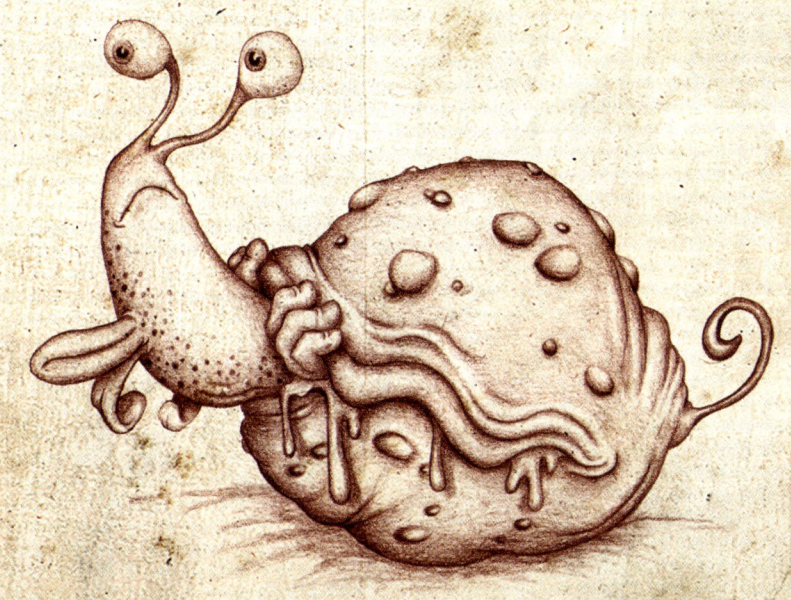

ENORMOUSLY swollen and dribbling green funk
His Highness's nostrils were crusted with gunk.
His eyes were as red as the reddest red thing
and his tongue was all coated in filmy wet string.
His belly was growling like something ferocious.
It burbled and tooted. The stink was atrocious.

The throne room was splattered with all that remained
of the king's luncheon feast and the things it contained.
Feathers and bones and jars, cups, and entrails,
melon rinds, gristles, and forks, beaks, and fish scales,
snail shells and dishes and napkins in tatters
talons and toenails and gravy-stained platters.

In the midst of the mess, on a throne worn and crummy
His Majesty writhed and clutched at his tummy.
Sweat dripped from his forehead and dampened his pits.
His cheeks were all ruddy and peppered with zits.
A pitiful whimper crawled up from his gizzard.
He coughed and he mumbled, "Come closer, my wizard."

"I'm sicker than sick," said the king with a groan.
"From dining on things that were best left alone."
He hacked and he puked and he beckoned me near.
I covered my nose as he belched in my ear.
His breath was a reek like the foulest cologne.
And he said, "If you cure me I'll give you my throne."

Because I'm a wizard with wizardly flair
I jumped around waving my wand in the air
and chanting and shouting, attracting strange looks
and reading from scrolls and all sorts of odd books.
I fed him unguents and potions and painted him green
I shaved off his hair and I tinctured his spleen.

But nothing was working. He'd had quite enough
of arcane hocus-poking and mystical guff.
And I, with my wand and my tall pointy hat
and all of bags of arcane this and that
could not find a cure for the king's ill condition.
Was I a great wizard or a common magician?

This thought vexed me greatly since I often boast
of the notion my magic is better than most.
So sadly that evening, the task unfulfilled,
I contacted Murgel, the head of my guild.
Murgel was wily, he knew what to do.
He sent me a cookbook and said, "Make some stew."

I dashed to the throne, to the king in his chair
I told him, "Don't worry. No need to despair."
His Highness's eyebrows wormed with frustration.
His bowels issued forth an absurd crepitation.
He belched and he moaned as I told him the scoop:
"My Lord, what you need is ALPHABEAST SOUP."

I summoned some minions. I conjured a troop
to fetch all the stuff I would need for the soup.
I already owned a big pot and utensils
for cooking the stew, but I needed essentials.
What I had to do next was gather a lot
of features of creatures to throw in the pot.

The recipe book was very specific.
The way of the cooking was quite scientific.
I couldn't just botch it and toss stuff in there
it had to be done with a great deal of care
in alphabeastical order, a task philosophic
the results of a failure could be catastrophic.

I read the book thrice and I fashioned a list
which I gave to my minions and said, "Here's the gist:
Each of you take a big chunk of this letter
then bring back the goods and we'll make the king better.
Travel the world, search each cave, swamp, and pile
but be sure to proceed in alphabeastical style!"

"Alphabeastical style?" They said, "What's that mean?
Should we write on them, read to them, color them green?"
Now, my minions aren't stupid (well, some of them be)
so I said, "In the manner of A, B, C, D...
That's how you assemble the pieces, you see.
You can't go about things haphazardously."

The ABYSSAL AGONKUS, a beast so extreme
it inhabits volcanoes and bathes in hot steam,
was the first on the list and we needed some scales
from the scalps of its heads and the tips of its tails.
A minion named Gorance, assigned to this task
said, "*How should I get them?*" I answered, "*Just ask.*"

The scraggly hairs on a BOZZLE'S backside
are longer than those on the rest of its hide.
They're pointy and bristly and wiry and dry
and if you're not careful they'll poke out your eye.
The soup called for bristles, about two or three,
so I ordered Pogford to tweeze some for me.

In an insect-plagued swamp, by the light of six moons
I sent my man Oogle to scoop with his spoons
from the ear of a CHONK a thick, waxy accretion
and from it's left nostril a noxious secretion.
He accomplished the task but expressed his distaste
at fouling his spoons with such bodily waste.

Three minions, all brothers dressed up in disguise,
gathered some tears from a lovesick DORP'S eyes.
The task wasn't easy. It was kind of a scandal,
almost too much for three brothers to handle.
I'll spare you their plan. Let's just say it consisted
of stilts and a dress and a wig they enlisted.

Grunkle, a minion who's good at spelunking,
I sent underground in search of a gunk ring.
A gunk ring is made when ELMOPAS respond
with a song to the wag of an ERGICKLE'S frond.
The Ergickle, in turn, waves its frond all around
decorating the cave with a luminous mound.

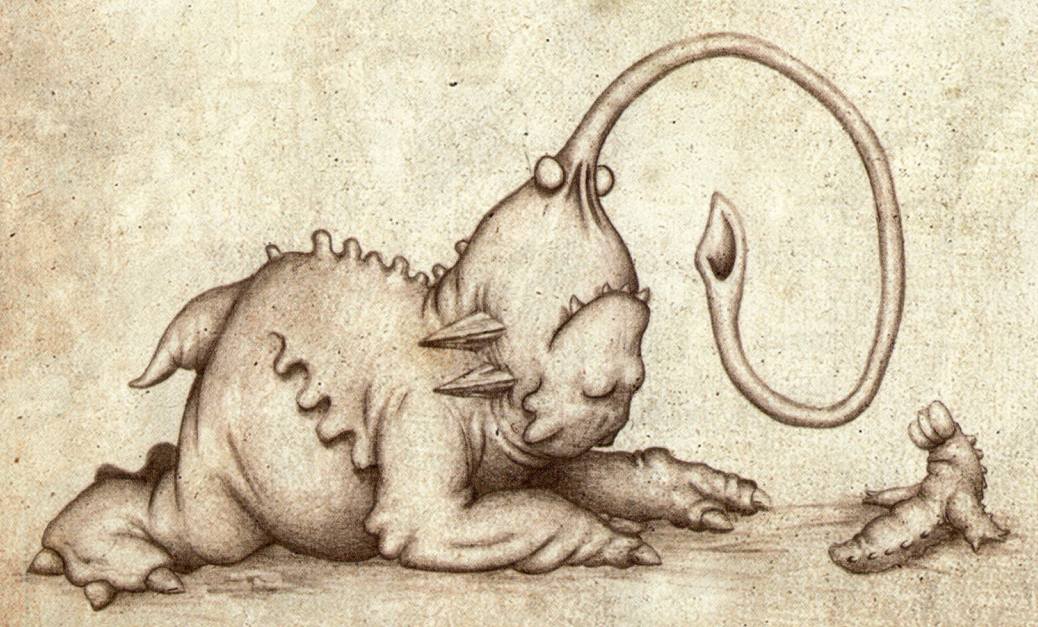

In a flowery jungle, way up in the twigs
a beast called the FLOUNCE dines on nuts, bugs, and figs.
The thing about Flounces that makes people wary
is they're awfully cute but their toenails are scary.
They're long, curved, and wicked with venomous drippings
so Bonzo wore gloves when collecting the clippings.

On a bleak lanky spire in inclement weather
Puckle the minion purloined a huge feather
from the wing of a GUMP-WUMP, the world's loudest bird,
the most cacophonous caller that's ever been heard.
It shrieks and it whistles; it cackles and huffs.
That's why Puckle's mom packed three pairs of earmuffs.

On a powdery beach near the far western shore
four minions thought thoughts never thought of before,
like, "How do we swipe the mustache off the grin
of a dagger-mouthed HOOPH while still wearing our skin?"
Three out of four found the answer quite fleeting
so Hassafrass ran while the Hooph sat there eating.

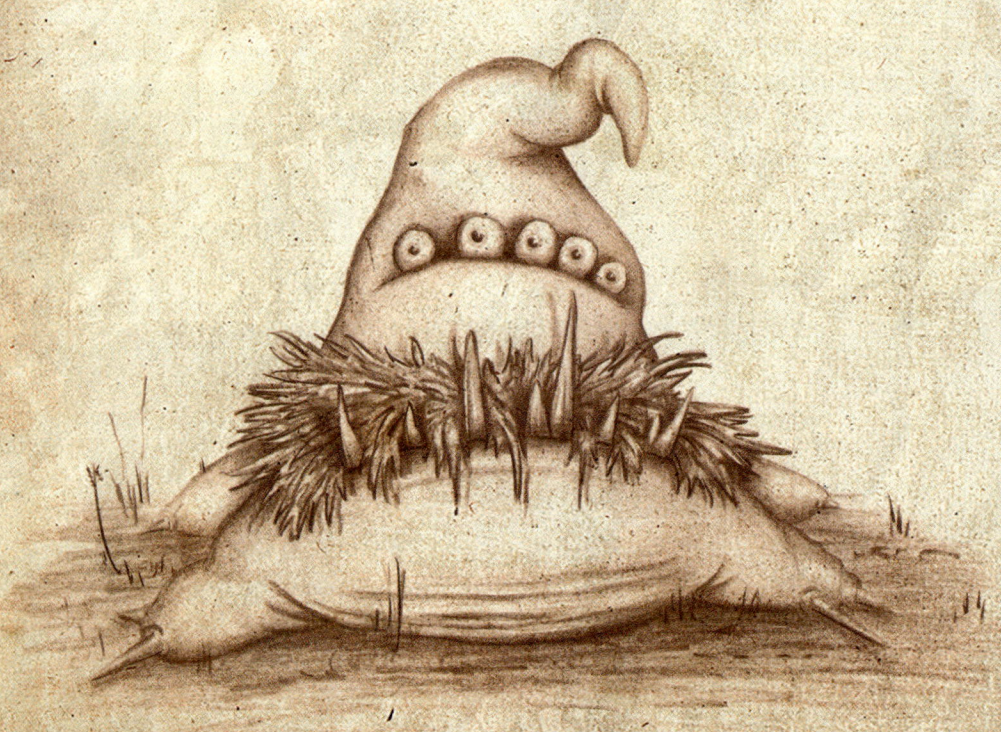

Deep in the depths of the deepest deep ocean
a fish called an IGG makes the strangest commotion.
It waggles its fins and exudes a thick sludge
that sticks fish together (they can't even budge).
The soup called for some of this fish-sludgey flotsam
so a minion named Alvin dove down and he got some.

Equipped with a clothespin, two gloves and some tongs
an unfortunate minion prepared for the throngs
of stenches and ichors and reeks that exude
from the buns of a **JOFFLE-O-NINECHEEKS** pursued.
He cornered the beast in a market bazaar.
You **DO NOT** want to know what he put in his jar.

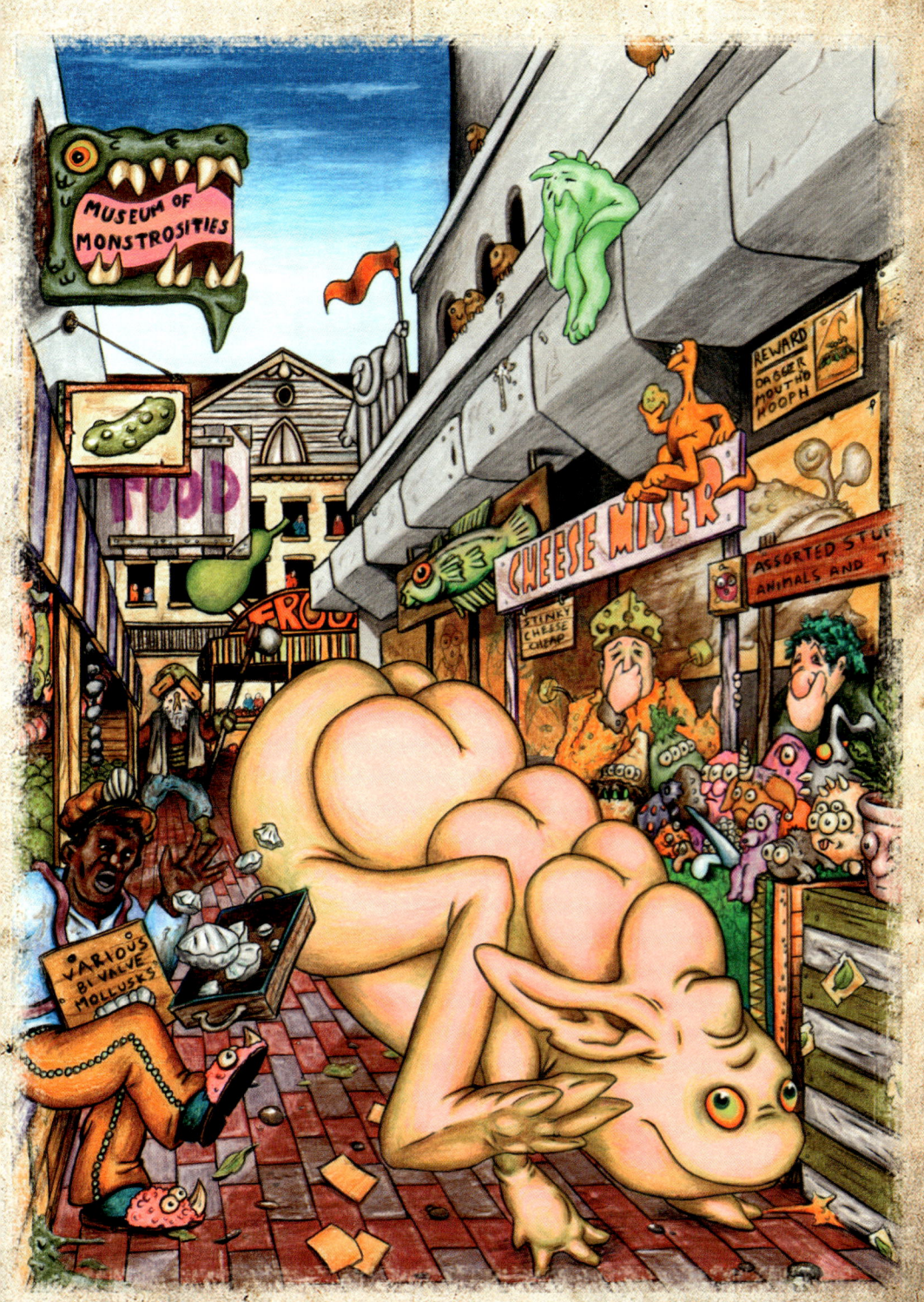

The KOLOB of Krofe, a cantankerous creature
has the world's driest scalp (and that's its best feature).
So knowing this knowledge and needing some flakes
a minion named Morris proceeded with rakes
to harvest the noggin of this scurfy critter
and collect the dandruff in a waterproof gitter.

The green-speckled LUMO lives in symbiosis
with a thing called a LUMPHUS with rank halitosis.
The Lumo, it's known, cleans the Lumphus's gums,
scraping off tartar and picking out crumbs.
The Lumo, in turn, earns a pittance or two
selling crumb-tartar cookies (I bought three for the stew).

Murble the minion, in raincoat and boots
and umbrella and crossbow (to settle disputes),
went in search of the MOON-KISS who's often found thriving
near waterfalls, cliff sides, and places for diving.
Its detachable tail forms a leash of a sort
that keeps it from squishing when diving for sport.

In a hole in the ground near some lush veggie patches
The nerdulous NURDLE itches and scratches.
It's body is covered in brilliant red blisters
(an allergic reaction it shares with its sisters).
The Nurdle did not put up much of a fuss
when we popped a few blisters and gathered the pus.

Opo the Sog was a minion with guts.
He was bold, brave, and strong and a little bit nuts.
When I tasked him with milking some milk from the udder
of an OMPUS and churning the stuff into butter
"I'm your man," Opo smiled, "I'm strong and I'm brave."
I wonder what flowers he'd like on his grave.

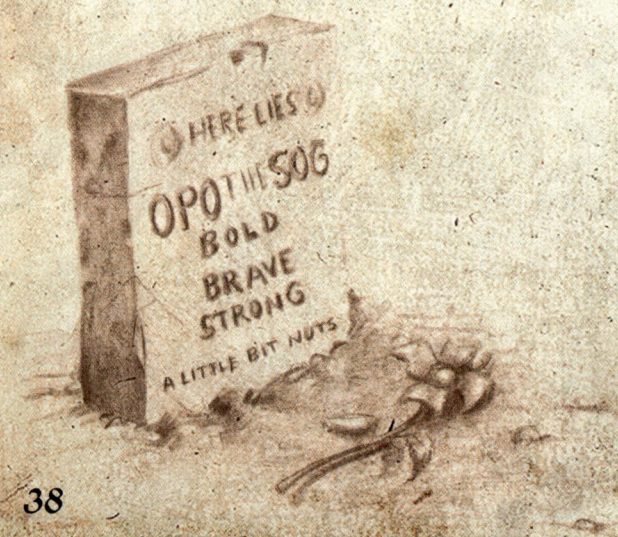

In a crystalline pond in a tall bamboo grove
lives a beast called the PRONK who sits guarding its trove
of treasures and baubles and shiny pink gall stones
it coughs up each night after dining on skull bones.
These stones aren't just pretty, they're valuable too
as a vital component of alphabeast stew.

A beast called a QUOOP in a nest in a tree
on top of a hill overlooking the sea
sings a song so delightful it's known to incite
rain in the desert and sunshine at night.
My most musical minions examined the Quoop
While I pondered how to put song in a soup.

Next on the list was a sort of a grease
that congeals 'tween the folds on the guts of obese
creatures called RUNCIDS that gorge on the seeds
and flowers that blossom on night-blooming weeds.
In turn the grease drippings are used by the plants
to polish their leaves and attract tasty ants.

Locked in the dungeon of the castle I dwell in
lives Ribar the Rage, a malevolent felon.
He's jailed in a cell eating water and bread
with a beast called a SOULSLURP who lives in his head.
It feeds on the madness it finds in his dreams
and excretes only vapors and lunatic screams.

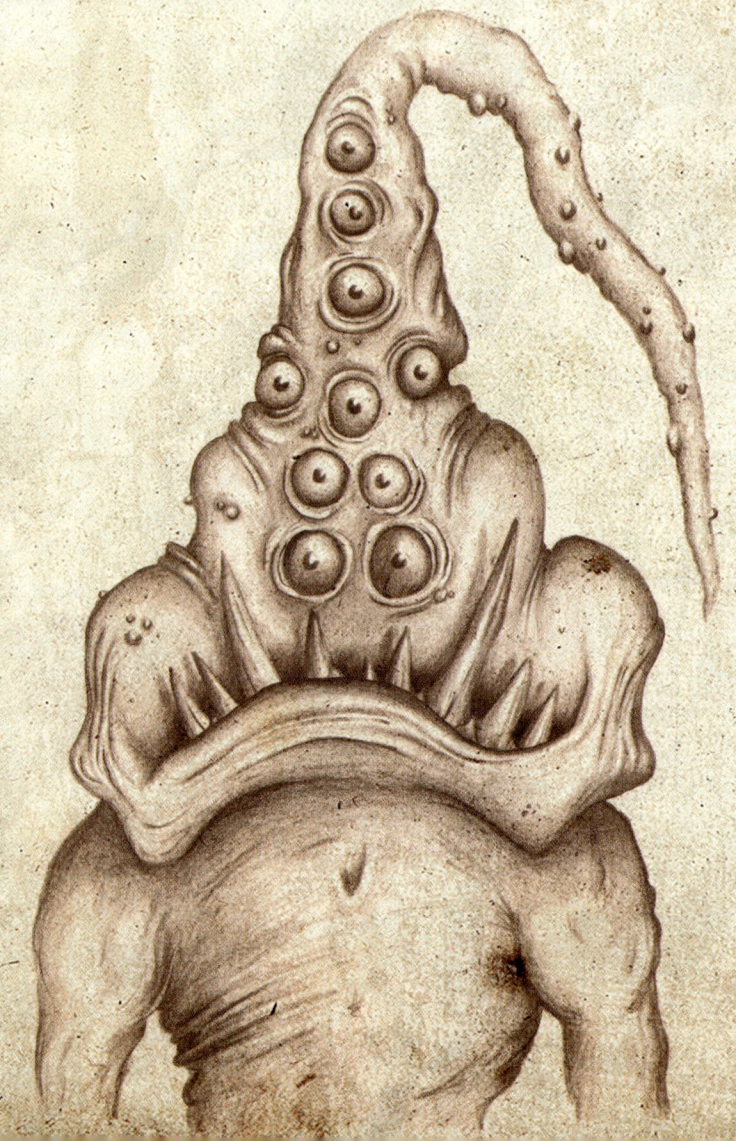

47

The drool of a **TOBBLE** is viscous and thick
and allows it to pull off a difficult trick.
By swinging on vines of gelatinous froth,
an ingredient needed for alphabeast broth,
the Tobble can flee from its foes and my minion.
It's real hard to catch if you want my opinion.

Icicles, snowballs, and igloos abound
in the land where the frost-lurking UBBUBB is found.
It's luscious eyelashes keep snowflakes from getting
into its eyes while it spends its days sledding
down ice-covered mountains and snowy hillsides
on a toboggan it made out of fresh minion hides.

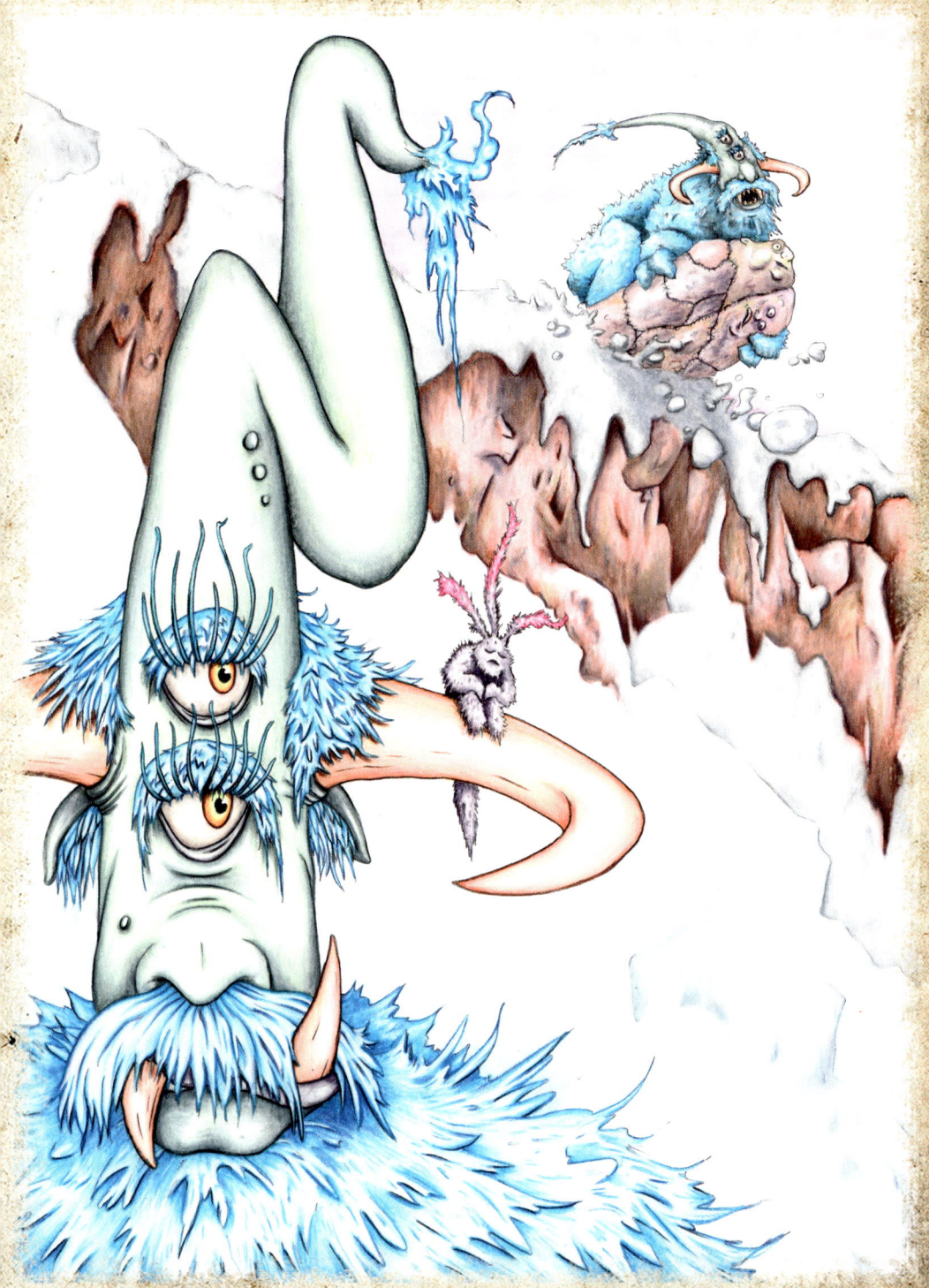

In a foul boggy fen with a stench most revolting
a minion named Meg fetched a shed VASCAL molting.
The Vascal, it's known, has a skin tough and scaly
that sloughs from the rascal not once, but twice, daily.
Each morning and night at precisely six thirty
it grows a new skin when the old one gets dirty.

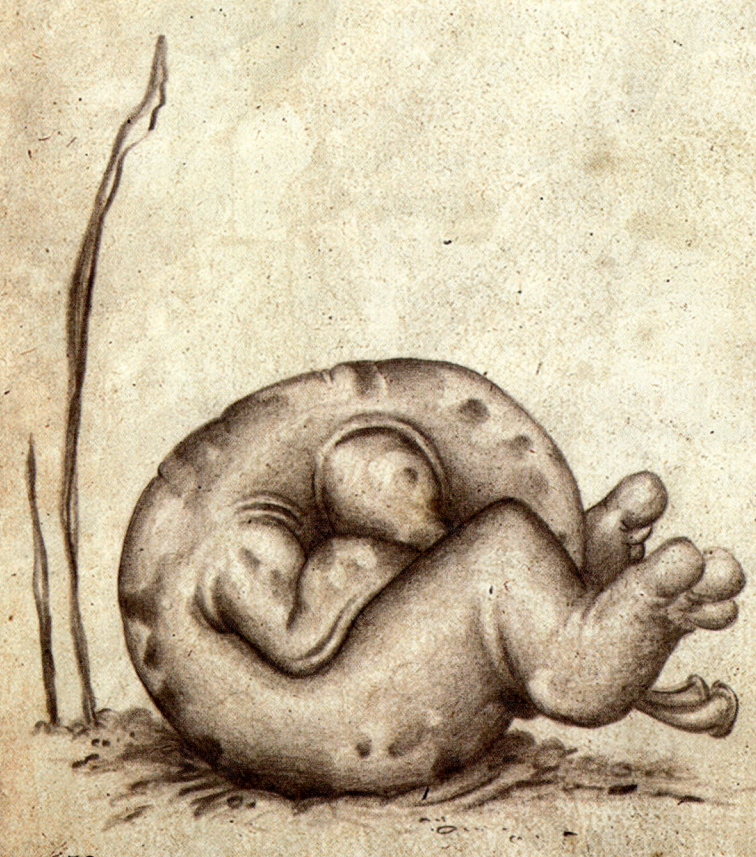

This next beast, the poet Folgomphus once wrote,
"...has the sun in its gizzard and gold in its throat."
But it isn't the song of the WOMPUS that's prized.
Instead its the phlegm in its gullet, comprised
of equal parts emeralds and moonbeams and goop.
We scrounged just a smidgen to put in the soup.

When a XIXI goes potty it's a happy affair,
for its tinkle smells lightly of apple and pear.
The soup called for a dose of this sweet golden flow
(it's part of the croûton, to soften the dough).
Gordo the minion tracked the beast to a tunnel
and chased after it with a cup and a funnel.

With a snore that's so raucous it shatters the ground
and a navel renowned as the deepest around
the YOPP, when it snores, snores its snores in a crypt.
So I sent my man Brumpus to the graveyard equipped
with a snorkel, a pole, a string, hook and some stuff
to fish in the Yopp's belly button for fluff.

Lastly I needed just one more component
and this final beast was the toughest opponent.
My men went to gather some sweat from the brow
of the deadliest monster the law will allow.
A beast called the ZUMTHO, with ten thousand horns
lots of teeth, fifty arms, and tails covered in thorns.

Not to mention it's tentacles, spines, and its jaws,
and the fact that each arm has about ninety claws.
And that's not the worst thing, not even by far,
nor is the fact that its tongues are bizarre
big pickles of flesh all dripping with toxin
and its cheeks are like pouches it stores giant rocks in

then spits them at minions like petrified rain
while its eyes spin in circles to drive them insane.
No, the worst thing about the Zumtho is its breath.
It's sort of an acidic ice cloud of death
with poison and fire and thick rancid smoke
and lightning and needles and stuff to invoke

soggy trousers and fear in the bravest of guys
who run away screaming with tears in their eyes.
Despite all the horror, they managed to get
a rag near its brow which they swabbed with its sweat.
Then the minions ran screaming (those few who survived)
to my tower with soup-stuff and when they arrived...

I took all the fixings and dashed to the galley
my mind focused on the impending finale.
Picture me on the throne, all fancy and grand,
the world's greatest wizard and king of the land.
That's what'll happen once the soup does it's thing:
the king will be healthy and I will be king.

With cauldrons and kettles and pots, pans, and blades
and cooks and cook's helpers and scullery maids
and forks and spoons and ladles and vessels
and alembics, decanters and mortars and pestles
and spices and veggies and onions and shrooms
and tomatoes, potatoes, and peppers and blooms

and pollen from flowers and also their petals
and stinkweed and skunkweed and chopped stinging nettles
and oil and water and barley and lard
and all sorts of other stuff scrounged from the yard
I worked for three days or maybe for nine
concocting concoctions and brewing the brine

and every few minutes, or at least once a while,
I rechecked the cookbook and sorted the pile
of secretions and drippings and hairs, nails, and goop
and other stuff gathered to put in the soup.

When it was ready I set it to boil
on a stove filled with coals, wood, and hot flaming oil
and lava and embers and combustible gases
and reeds, herbs and spices and sweet-smelling grasses.
And while it sat bubbling for three days and an hour
I chanted out loud the proscribed words of power:

A is for Agonkus whose scales form the base
when rendered with Yopp fluff to make a thick paste.

B is for Bozzle whose bristles are nice
for cleansing the palette and cutting the spice.

C is for Chonk with waxes that thicken
the broth with a flavor they say tastes like chicken.

D is for Dorp whose tears add a glint
of happiness, romance and longing and mint.

E is for Elmopas and also Ergickle
whose gunk adds a funk like a nine year old pickle.

F is for Flounce whose toenails add crunch
when roasted and seasoned and grouped in a bunch.

G is for Gump-wump whose feather's applied
to stir up the broth so it doesn't get fried.

H is for Hooph with a mustache so furry
you blend it with oil to make a fur slurry.

I is for Igg whose sludge adds a reek
of fish heads and fish guts and fishy physique

J is for Joffle who adds to the soup
something unpleasant that might rhyme with soup.

K is for Kolob whose dry flaky head
provides dandruff and dander to flavor the spread.

L is for Lumo and Lumphus (those two)
whose tartar-crumb cookies add chunks to the stew.

M is for Moon-kiss whose detachable tail
is used to scrub clean every pot, bowl, and pail.

N is for Nurdle with pus clear and runny
that sweetens the soup with a tang like fresh honey.

O is for Ompus whose curd thick and sour
infuses the stew with Ompus milk power

P is for Pronk whose gall calculi
add sparkle and twinkle and spit in your eye.

Q is for Quoop whose song gives the stew
a slight touch of whimsy and passion and rue.

R is for Runcid whose thick sloppy grease
adds feelings of lechery, lust and caprice.

S is for Soulslurp who feeds on a dream
whose vapors provide us with flavorful steam

T is for Tobble whose drool adds a bit
of ickiness, stickiness, laughter and spit.

U is for Ubbubb whose eyelashes add
a flavor of paisley and checkers and plaid.

V is for Vascal who gives us shed skin
to add to the soup an unwelcome chagrin.

W is for Wumpus, the wily rascal
whose phlegm rids us of the chagrin of the Vascal.

X is for Xixxi whose tinkle we use
to soften the crouton and flavor infuse.

Y is for Yopp whose fluff from the belly
makes the soup aromatic and pungent and smelly.

Z is for Zumtho whose sweat does the trick
of ensuring the soup makes the eater less sick.

In alphabeastical order the soup was completed.
The only thing left was to bowl it and eat it.
So here's what I did: I put the stew in a dish
then I went to the throne room to grant the king's wish.
And there the king sat, with a miserable groan
he glanced up at me and said "Leave me alone."

I said, "But Your Highness I'm here with the stew.
I think it will fix you. You'll be good as new.
Take a big bite now. Here, use this spoon.
Eat it for breakfast – feel better by noon."
The king raised an eyebrow, said something obscene,
then he sniffed at the soup in the silver tureen.

He clutched the spoon weakly with faltering grip,
bent his lips forward and slurped the first sip.
He let out a shriek like he'd licked a hot coal
then he threw down the spoon and he picked up the bowl.
His eyes were on fire, his cheeks were alight,
then he drained the whole vessel in one mighty bite.

In just a few minutes (I noticed discreetly)
all the king's symptoms had cleared up completely.
It worked! He was better; the soup did its thing!
The king was now healthy and I was the king!
That's at least what I thought, but to my despair,
the king said, "Thanks wizard, now come get your chair."

He stepped from the throne and sneered, "Take it. It's yours.
It's old and it's worn and it gives me bedsores.
The gold's lost its luster, the gems are all dull,
the cushions are flattened, the seat is too small,
the legs are uneven and the hinges all squeak
so I'm having a new one delivered next week."

Just a chair? That's not fair! I thought I would rule!
Instead of a king I was tricked like a fool.
His Majesty duped me to heal him with stew
after all of the excrement, slobber and goo...
I went to my tower to plan my attack...

Next time

THE ALPHABEAST SOUP

will bite back!